7 DEADLY SINS

CRISTINA TORRES

iUniverse LLC
Bloomington

SEVEN DEADLY SINS

iUniverse books may be ordered through booksellers or by contacting:

iUniverse LLC
1663 Liberty Drive
Bloomington, IN 47403
www.iuniverse.com
1-800-Authors (1-800-288-4677)

Because of the dynamic nature of the Internet, any web addresses or links contained in this book may have changed since publication and may no longer be valid. The views expressed in this work are solely those of the author and do not necessarily reflect the views of the publisher, and the publisher hereby disclaims any responsibility for them.

Any people depicted in stock imagery provided by Thinkstock are models, and such images are being used for illustrative purposes only. Certain stock imagery © Thinkstock.

ISBN: 978-1-4917-2092-9 (sc)
ISBN: 978-1-4917-2093-6 (e)

Library of Congress Control Number: 2014900593

Printed in the United States of America.

iUniverse rev. date: 01/22/2014

Dedicated to Phillip and Gloria.
Thank you for believing.

LUCIFER REMINISCES

If I were about to die, would you save me? If I were to bleed, would you heal me? If I were to call, would you come? If I were forgotten, would you remember me? If I were cast out, would you redeem me? If I were to leave, would you miss me?

How can you say that you love me and then leave me alone? How can you say that you forgive me and then leave me here? How can you say that everything will be all right when I feel empty? How can you expect me to change if I hurt? How can I live if everything dies?

I sit here by a river that was created long, long ago by him—him being God. But he is not my God. I tried to acknowledge the light and see it for its wondrous beauty, but alas, I failed. I must retreat into my domain, shut out all that was once good, and accept myself for who I am. I cannot be like you. I cannot live in a world filled with tranquility and the reassurance of people around me. I cannot believe in those I know and expect them to keep their words and promises. It's not possible to refrain from the negativity and hypocrisy that I see within life. There is far too much denial, hate, and corruption.

Well, that's not me. I was pulled out of the darkness, only to be disappointed with its effect on humanity, so it is my decision to no longer recognize humans for what they are: mortals who contradict each other more than demons do, but who are still forgiven of their sins.

But what about those of us who dwell deep within the dark, far from direct human contact? How are we to deal with this? I cannot be in the light, for it hurts me to see humans taking advantage of forgiveness. One day a sin is committed, and the following day the human enters a church and expects the priest or minister to lift and banish his sins. It has come to my attention that, after the sin has been lifted, such an individual just creates another sin—and this pattern is repeated over and over. How is this possible?

It isn't right for you to be hypocritical and continue the blasphemy of forgiveness, because sooner or later there will be a sin that is unforgivable, and then whom will you turn to? That is why I dwell far from hope and keep myself in my domain with those in my legion. We too once committed a sin so powerful that we were banished into another realm. Still, I do not really hate mankind. I do not always despise humans. I do not wish for their downfall, for I too have granted wishes to those who follow my beliefs, to those so desperate that they will compromise their greatest possession to satisfy themselves.

Humans are easily corrupted and can be easily manipulated into doing just about anything. I hate it when someone is within my reach—and then they convert in order to save themselves from me. Sometimes I interfere and stop them from achieving forgiveness. But I am not evil! I am not hate! I am not suffering! I am just misunderstood!

You cannot compare me to him or any other. I have powers of my own, and I have my favorites whom I watch constantly, but they do not see this. I see all and hear all. When mortals were created, there was a question of doubt, and soon enough, jealousy was created and favoritism was revealed. He chose mortals over his creation.

He created man and still favors man to this day. He has a soft spot for mankind and is constantly willing to forgive. Mortals are tested on a daily basis, and I too like to test and create roadblocks. Sometimes I need to test those who are considered holy or peaceful or the few who are committed to their religious beliefs. This needs to be done to test their faith. On occasion, some fail and stray from their religious ways, and a few are born atheist. So I have decided to meet with an archangel. You see, I have an idea, and I believe it will prove what I have come to believe: that mortal hearts are easily influenced and can change at any given time. No prize is really needed, but it would make my idea a bit more interesting and amusing.

I do not wish for outside interference from the archangels or any religious forms, so I need to call a meeting with one of the head archangels in order to prove my point, but first I need to have my idea acknowledged by "him." I cannot have any interference in this. It is a plan that I have been working on for some time, and I think the time has finally come to prove what I've been thinking all along.

Most humans commit sins on a daily basis, as I said, but some sins are deadly, and I must rely on those sins to fulfill my desire. I rule in the desolate wasteland of fire and brimstone. I have conducted every form of pain ever known.

I have punished a few with a repetition of death, and believe me: there is a lake of fire, and it burns constantly. You will find that being with me has its downside, and yet there is still the promise of serving me. I have my own scouts and my own legion, and it is their job to keep watch on mortals.

My role in your life isn't meant to scare you but to get you to understand that, yes, I exist. I am very much alive and real. I have seen many mortals pledge their lives to me. Then, within a few years, they abandon me and flee to him. And then I ask myself how it is possible that he can forgive just about anything—and especially those who have turned on him.

I wonder sometimes why he cares so much for his human creation. What is it that makes him so determined to save and accept them? That is something I will never understand. He once loved *us* so much that he spoke with us on a daily basis, and we were considered his greatest creation. Now, mortals have replaced us, and from what I hear, mortals call upon the angels for help when they need something.

I wonder how God feels about that. This is a complex world. Good and evil are constantly fighting and searching for souls. He searches for souls that can be redeemed. I search for souls that have given up all hope. Yes, there is a balance between us, but sometimes I wish I could have more leverage, because he is constantly winning. More and more humans are turning away from me, and I find myself losing a battle. Just when I think I have a human that is twisted, dark, and malicious, this human believes that his death is near, and soon he begs and wishes for deliverance from me. Within days I am forgotten.

Moments like these upset me, and if my plan works and certain influences are cast aside, I will be able to see what really happens during those crucial moments of death and life. The hour is near when I must prepare for the archangel's arrival. Soon, very soon, all doubt and uncertainty will be set aside, and we shall see which side really does triumph in the quest for the damnation or salvation of a human soul.

I can still remember when he held conversations with me, when I was considered his favorite, when he listened to what I had to say—until he created man. After that, I often asked to speak with him but was denied. He had no time for me. He spent all his time keeping a watchful eye on his creation, making sure they had everything they needed. He kept an eye on their transformation and adaptation in their new surroundings.

How could this be possible? How could he spend countless hours visualizing them, planning words of consultation and explanation for his new creation? I guess you could say that I felt abandoned, and in those moments of being denied, I began to feel hate for humans and resentment toward him.

He never fully explained his purpose in creating man, only that he was in love with his creation. Word began to spread among the angels that he had given man a soul—a soul! Now, that upset me even more, because it gave humans access to him after death. This would allow humans to enter the kingdom and meet with their Creator. Where did that leave the rest of us? I soon began to feel that I was no longer needed.

He had everything he wanted. He had his humans and he'd given them souls. He created a beautiful paradise for their survival. But what did he offer us?

We gained nothing from his creation. In fact, we lost what was most important to me. We lost him, and I knew that when we were abandoned and forgotten, things in heaven would change for us. There was a time when he did have us watching the humans interact with each other, but then he warned us not to involve ourselves with the flesh of mankind. We could never have intercourse or hold conversations with humans. We were denied all forms of encounter, but he still wanted us to keep a watch on them.

I had questions of my own that I wanted to ask humans, but it was forbidden. Then I had an idea. What if I could manipulate a human into doing my bidding? Would he still love them? Would he still refer to them as his greatest creation? How would it make him feel? Being who I was, I decided to test out this theory.

I manipulated his precious human. I convinced this human to do my bidding, and it worked. Word later spread in heaven that I had done it. I knew I had found a flaw in his creation. I had discovered a weakness in humans, and that angered him. It bothered him that I had been right. He had made a mistake in his creation.

How ironic it was that he only wished to speak with me when I caused commotion! There I stood in his radiant presence, hoping he would comfort me and explain his purpose for his creation, but instead he was very angry that I had interfered. His words to me were loving and disapproving at the same time. I argued with him and pleaded for an answer to my question. I will never forget what he said. He said he didn't need to explain his purpose for anything he created or destroyed. He did what he did, and we were never to question or doubt anything he said or did.

I felt anger. Not only had he refused to answer my question, but now it was clear that everything he did was for a reason—and none of us would ever know what that reason was. There shouldn't be secrets between us, I said to him. I'd thought we were all equal. I'd thought *we* were his greatest creation, not the humans!

I remember him looking at me and saying that we were *not* equal, that he was my father, that he had created me and could easily destroy me.

Was there no trust between us? I asked him.

He looked me straight in the eyes and said that I had broken his trust. I had broken his rule when I'd convinced his precious human to do my bidding, and that was wrong.

I turned my back on him and said that he was angry because I'd found a flaw in his creation. I told him that this bothered him because it meant that he wasn't perfect.

He looked at me and said that, because of my insolent words, I would no longer be by his side. I would no longer dwell there with him, because he was casting me out.

I looked at him and demanded to know why. He told me that I did not belong there, for I questioned everything he did. He said he could not allow me to stay there with doubt in my heart. He would not destroy me but would use me for another purpose. He would create a whole new world for me and see if I could still manipulate humans from there.

To this day, I am still there. I was made king—king and lord of the underworld, which most humans identify as hell or hades.

Since then, I have never spoken to him face-to-face. Most of the time, I receive messages through other archangels who continue to serve him. But what he didn't realize was that he gave me power. By casting me out, he gave me an opportunity to get closer to mortals. I live not only in my world but in theirs as well. I can easily transport myself anywhere here on earth and mingle with humans. I can appear to humans in the form of apparitions or miracles.

But today—today I'm here to meet with one of his archangels. This angel's name is Michael. He is very powerful and is one of the commanders on his angelic army. I have a proposition to offer.

Sitting here by the lake reminds me of when I first encountered my reflection after being cast out. It took me awhile to adapt to my transformation and to accept my new life. As I stare in the water, a new reflection is revealed. Something bright is coming in my direction, and that can only mean one thing. Michael is here, and I shall meet him halfway.

Chapter 1

LOST

"Somewhere in the depths of the underworld lies a forbidden place, and in that place there is a ruler—a ruler so powerful that his very name strikes fear into the hearts of men. Many doubt his existence, but he is real. He has many powers. One is the gift of persuasion, and another is the gift of illusions. He especially uses these on men." Father Leon pauses to write the name *Lucifer* on the chalkboard. "I hope you are all paying attention," he says. "This is very important."

Adam, a student in this sermon class, begins to daydream. He slowly falls into a deep sleep and begins to snore. His friend and fellow classmate Charlie taps him on the back and tells him to wake up. Hearing the sound of someone whispering, Father Leon turns to look at the class. Slowly he begins to make his way to the back of the room. Charlie taps harder. "Adam, wake up." Seeing this, Father Leon walks faster.

"As I was saying," Father Leon continues, "it has been said that one woman can send many men into hell. I know that many of you doubt me, but believe me, all it takes is her looks. As the expression goes, 'looks can kill.' Lucifer is known to disguise himself." Arriving at the back of the classroom, he finds Adam sleeping and yells, "Is this lecture really that boring?"

Adam awakens rapidly and begins to apologize. "Forgive me, Father Leon. It wasn't my intention to fall asleep in class. Please continue. I promise you, it won't happen again."

"You're right. It won't happen again, because you need to leave my class right now."

"What do you mean, I have to leave?"

"Leave!"

Furious, Father Leon walks back to the front of the class and continues teaching. Adam gets up and looks at Charlie.

"Why didn't you wake me?"

"I tried," says Charlie.

"Charlie!" shouts Father Leon. "Pay attention. This information will be part of next week's quiz."

Looking at Father Leon angrily, Adam pleads to stay. Father Leon turns his back and ignores him. Frustrated, Adam grabs his books, walks to the front of the room, and looks at Father Leon. "You know, you can't be right all the time. You can't possibly have all the answers for every situation we might encounter." Without responding, Father Leon continues his lecture. Adam angrily slams the door on his way out.

"This isn't fair."

Looking around, he walks to the courtyard and sits on a bench. He begins looking at his textbooks and takes a deep breath. "This is all because of you." He grabs his book of Bible verses and tosses it aside. "I can't do this!" he yells in frustration. Looking at his Bible, he begins to think about his life. How is it possible, he wonders, that one misfortune can turn into a lie that just keeps growing? Most of his family, and especially his mom, have pushed him into joining the monastery. It has always been her dream to see one of her children become a servant of the Lord.

But this isn't what Adam wants. He wants to live and explore, and most of all, he wants a family of my own. He feels that he has lost his freedom through no choice of his own. He is fulfilling his mother's dream, not his. He has never wanted to be part of the monastery, and the headmaster knows this.

Throughout his education, he has had to devote countless hours to memorizing Bible verses and praying constantly. He barely passes any classes. He knows he can never live a life of helping others. He would panic.

And how could he live with himself, knowing the sins that people committed? If he were to meet with someone before Mass and then see him during the service, he would dwell on the content of their conversation. That could mess up the service, and he would lose members of the church congregation. This is his biggest fear.

He has to face the fact that he is not meant to do this. It makes him sad, because he feels like he has failed—not just himself but God as well. Sometimes he lies in bed and thinks of the crucifixion. He wonders how one symbol can be so powerful.

Adam pauses and looks at his watch. He realizes that class will be over soon. "I don't want anyone to see me," he says to himself. "I have no choice. I have to leave the monastery."

Chapter 2

ENCOUNTER: THE MEETING

Like a shooting bullet, Lucifer descends from the sky, knocking the angel onto the ground. The angel angrily rises from the ground and yells at Lucifer. "Lucifer, is that any way to greet an old associate?"

Lucifer gives the angel a hesitant glance. "Michael, it's been a while."

Not trusting Lucifer, Michael stands opposite him and says, "You still haven't changed your arrogant ways."

Half grinning, Lucifer says, "I'm not arrogant, just misunderstood."

Michael looks at Lucifer angrily. "Doesn't matter. You're still evil and transparent. Speak your business."

Lucifer slowly begins to walk toward Michael. "I have a proposition to make. I want to test a mortal."

"You and I know that mortals are tested every day," says Michael.

"Yes, and every time they are tested, they are soon forgiven for their sins," says Lucifer angrily.

Michael begins to walk around Lucifer. "Don't tell me it bothers you that they are still out of your reach. Don't you understand yet? Sooner or later, many humans find themselves going back to what's good, back to what is expected of them, and they turn away from you and rejoice with my Lord God."

Lucifer stops Michael and looks him straight in the eyes. "What bothers me, Michael, is that he can forgive all mortals for their sins—even the deadliest of them—and that is not right. They should be denied forgiveness and given to me."

"No, what bothers you is that there is still hope and salvation for humans, so state your purpose."

Taking a step back, Lucifer opens his eyes wide and speaks with an evil grin. "Michael, it's like I said. I want to test a mortal—not just any mortal, but a mortal with a good heart. I want to see if your God will forgive a mortal who has committed all seven deadly sins within a twenty-four-hour period, and I want no interference from any archangel, angel, saint, priest, pastor, or minister."

Michael shakes his head. "So what you're saying is that you want no religious encounter at all."

"Exactly—and especially from God himself. I want to push this mortal, and I can't do it if someone or something holy interferes."

Michael changes his expression and asks seriously, "What does God get out of this? What are the terms?"

Seeing the serious expression on Michael's face, Lucifer explains his plan. "If, during the twenty-four-hour period, the mortal does not recognize God, and his soul is corrupted to the point of non-redemption, I want it. I want that mortal soul myself. This should prove that not all humans should be forgiven."

Disappointed, Michael looks up at Lucifer. "What if the human remembers God while committing all seven deadly sins? What happens then?"

Lucifer approaches Michael angrily. "I will stop influencing mortals on my own and will let them decide for themselves whether they are good or evil. I will not interfere in their transformation during their life spans."

"If you remember," Michael says, "God does not make deals, especially with you, so I don't think he will consider your proposal."

Lucifer rubs his hands together and looks at the ground. "This is important to me. If he denies me this opportunity, I shall find another way to prove my point."

Not sure of what to think," Michael asks suspiciously, "And what would that point be?"

Lucifer yells, "That not all sins are forgivable!"

Michael thinks for a second before shaking his head. "I highly doubt that he's willing to do this."

Lucifer gives him an evil glare. "Just ask him. You know I can't ask him myself. He never speaks to me, especially after centuries of being cast out."

"Very well," says Michael, "but I expect that he will decline your offer. I shall return in a while with your answer, but don't get your hopes up. Remember that God makes deals with no one—especially you."

Lucifer watches Michael as he takes flight and soars out of sight. Walking back to the river, Lucifer decides to use it to find his chosen human. He sees many humans he could choose for his test.

"There are so many different types of humans in the world," he says to himself. "Choosing one will be a difficult task. How is it possible that there seems to be more good than evil? I must find the balance between both forces in order to find my human." He glares at male mortals in the reflection of the river. "I believe my only opportunity lies in a male human, for males seem much easier to influence than females, and males are very competitive within their own species. They are blinded by lust and greed. Some men even thirst for blood. They crave war and violence. I believe it makes them feel more dominant."

Lucifer waves his hand over the river to reveal females. "The female gender seems to be less interested in bloodshed, but like the males, they too can have a change of heart. I have studied both sexes. They are equal when it comes to desperation and deceit. Both can be influenced, and I believe my first influence was over a female."

Lucifer rises and walks toward a tree. He feels hate and rage. "I despise humans for what they are—insolent fools that have no idea whatsoever that their only value is in their souls." He controls his anger and remembers his followers. "Sometimes my followers have offerings in my name, and I praise them for that brief moment of silence in the air. It's important that the offerings have meaning. The spoken words have to be heartfelt as well as from the soul. Only then will I be present to observe my so-called followers and give them praise for their loyalty."

Lucifer begins to think. Words cannot explain what he feels at that precise moment. He has mixed emotions about what God will say. He knows there is a slight chance that his request will be declined. After all, God feels betrayed.

Lucifer paces back and forth, unaware that Michael has arrived. "Lucifer," Michael says, "are you still blaming our Father for your miserable destruction?"

Lucifer turns and sees Michael staring at him from a distance. "Michael," he says, "you know it's not nice to sneak around."

Seeing Lucifer's reaction to his surprise visit, Michael walks toward the river. "Who would know better about this than you? Wasn't it you who snuck around first?"

Lucifer grins and walks toward Michael. "Same old Michael. You never forget anything. Well, what did he say?"

"First, tell me why this is so important to you. You know you will never win, so why not stop now?"

Lucifer yells angrily, "What did he say?"

Michael looks disappointed. "He's going to allow it, but only under certain circumstances."

Lucifer rubs his forehead in frustration. "What circumstances? I did not want him to set any rules or guidelines. This is my test, not his."

Michael places his hand on his sword and yells angrily, "If you want to do this, you're going to have some boundaries."

Lucifer interrupts Michael. "Boundaries! Whatever for? This is my test. He shouldn't interfere by changing or adding to my plan."

Forcefully Michael interrupts Lucifer. "It is his decision, and if you want to go forward with your plans, you'd better obey and listen to his proposal. If not, I can easily leave and tell him you are defiant and refuse to cooperate."

Taking a deep breath, Lucifer pauses for a minute and decides to listen to what Michael has been trying to tell him. "Fine, I'll listen. What are these circumstances?"

Calmly Michael moves his hand away from his sword. "This mortal must not be harmed in any way. His or her final cause of death cannot be inflicted by you. It has to come naturally."

Lucifer gives Michael a blank expression. "What are you saying?"

"The mortal cannot die after the seven sins are committed. Those are the circumstances. Either accept them or forget your test."

Lucifer shouts, "Forget it? Never! Very well, I shall make sure that the mortal I choose will not die by my hands after all seven sins are committed. But tell me, Michael, what did he say when I demanded no religious influences whatsoever?"

Michael stops smiling and wears a grim expression. "He laughed at first. He knows that whoever you choose will not forget him, so you really should quit now. As long as there are good souls in the world, you will never win."

Lucifer moves toward Michael. Michael sees him come closer and slowly takes a step back. "It's not about winning, Michael. It's about proving him wrong. This frightens you because, if I can do this, it could change the number of souls that enter heaven on a daily basis. Is that what you're afraid of—me gaining power over his precious humans?"

Michael steps toward Lucifer. "You have no such power. Every time a human strays from you, sooner or later they return like good little sheep and find their way back to God."

"This time things will be different," Lucifer says. "You'll see. I will prove my point, and I will win."

Michael looks Lucifer over from top to bottom. "You're still arrogant and hopeless," he says. "It's no wonder you were banned. You could never fit in. You were always the black sheep of the family because of your stubbornness in not following orders." Lucifer listens silently, and Michael continues. "Every time God did something wonderful for mankind, you were always the first to question, and that's blasphemy. Don't you remember what God said when we were created? I believe he said, 'Never question what I do.' But did you listen? No! You had to be different and speak your mind, and look where it got you."

Lucifer smiles at Michael. "I see nothing wrong with my current position. You seem to forget that I too have powers, dark powers that I can easily use to influence humans to doing my bidding." Lucifer opens his eyes wide. "I am feared as much as God is, so do not tell me I have no powers, because I do. If you can't see that, then you're blind."

Michael is cautious, knowing what Lucifer can do. He draws his sword.

Lucifer notices that Michael has pulled out his sword, but he continues talking and walks in circle around him. "I have created and unleashed among humans many forms of what you call evil—take the birth of the Antichrist, for example. It was my idea to create a mortal that would cause much havoc on earth. And don't you remember how many humans have already died by one hand—the hand that I guided—and the one mind that I controlled?"

Laughing, Lucifer continues. "It was I, if you recall, who sent millions flocking to your gates and caused corruption on earth. Boy, did I get God's attention then. Everyone was blaming me, and they were right. It was I, and it was worth it. One dark, evil, corrupted soul for thousands of others that had no purpose."

Michael interrupts angrily. "How can you say that? That's blasphemy."

"It does not matter, Michael," Lucifer responds. "I got the soul I wanted. Their deaths were worth my efforts, and I do not regret anything."

Michael looks sadly at Lucifer, stopping him in his tracks. "How can you be so cruel toward humans? Have you no pity?"

Lucifer looks Michael straight in the eyes and says, "No. Ever since I noticed a change in God and his attitude, I knew something was wrong. I knew we were no longer important."

Michael looks down with a disappointed expression. "Why do you think that way? He still loves you. You are just too blind to see it."

Shaking his head, Lucifer yells, "No, Michael! His love was only temporary. If you remember, I was banished and crowned king of the underworld. He put me in exile. Heaven is out of my reach."

Feeling sorry for Lucifer, Michael puts his sword away and places his hand on Lucifer's shoulder. "Lucifer, if you were to repent and show mercy toward humans, I'm sure he would forgive you."

Lucifer looks down for a second and then lifts his head and speaks doubtfully. "No, I don't need forgiveness. He turned his back on me long ago. I don't need him or anyone else, and I will never regret what I did. I have no reason to repent."

Slowly Michael removes his hand and shakes his head in disbelief. "Then you truly did lose your grace. You know, there was a time when I looked up to you, but now I despise you and all your work. All you do is cause corruption, hate, anger, and violence. You are the definition of evil, and because of your actions, you lost everything."

"Amuse me, Michael," says Lucifer. "Tell me, what did I lose when I gained power?"

Disappointed, Michael stands back and takes a final look at Lucifer before he leaves. "His love, Lucifer, his love. Now, if you will excuse me, I have to return to the kingdom where my Father of all creations lives." Michael takes flight.

Lucifer yells angrily at Michael as he leaves. "Your words have no effect on me! Do you hear me, Michael? No affect whatsoever!" Filled with loneliness, Lucifer begins to recall how betrayed he felt many centuries ago. "His love! It was his love that pushed me away. But it doesn't matter. I don't need him. He was never there for me. Still, his acceptance of my proposal makes me doubt myself. Why did he agree? He's up to something; I can feel it. Even though I have been cast out of heaven, we still have some kind of connection, but he refuses to acknowledge it."

Walking toward the river, Lucifer waves his hand over the water and sees the human he has chosen for his test. "It's almost noon, and yes, he seems like the perfect candidate for my project. All I need to do is find a way to begin. Let's see. What is it that humans need in order to survive? Money, of course! Without it, they have no way of life. Let's just see what happens when money is the object of his affection. This could be the key to unleashing all seven deadly sins.

Chapter 3

THE HUMAN: FAREWELL

Inside the convent, a tall, handsome man is packing his belongings into his backpack. Adam stands in front of his bed and takes a look around the room. With a sad smile, he remembers the Lord's Prayer and begins to recite it softly to himself. "Our Father, who art in heaven . . ." He is interrupted by Charlie, a pale man who exhibits the beauty of a saint.

"Adam, what are you doing?" asks Charlie.

Adam stops praying, takes a deep breath, and looks at Charlie. "I'm really going to miss this place," he says.

"Why? Where are you going? Why are you packing?" Concerned, Charlie puts his hand on Adam's backpack. "Are they sending you somewhere else?"

Adam opens the drawer in the nightstand and shakes his head. "I'm running away from the church."

"You're what?"

"I can't help but feel like I've failed in some way. I should have been more prepared."

Charlie walks toward him. "Adam, you don't need to do this. I think we should talk to the headmaster."

Frustrated, Adam thinks of a lie and interrupts Charlie. "No! I overheard Father Leon complaining about me. It's only a matter of time before I'm called in to the headmaster's office."

"You don't need to leave," Charlie says. "Let me help you."

"I dedicated many years of my life trying to serve God—and for what? Only to fail?"

"You shouldn't see it as failure. You can learn from this."

Adam pulls an item from a drawer. "Learn? Learn what? Charlie, there's no hope for me. I just have to face it. You know as well as I do that I don't belong here."

"Why would you say that? God brought you here for a reason. It's all part of his plan."

Adam pulls out an old crucifix made of green and black marble. "Here, Charlie. Take it."

"Your crucifix?"

"You can have it. I don't think I'm going to need it."

Charlie opens his eyes wide and looks at the crucifix. "But Adam . . ."

"Take it. It's too heavy for me to carry."

"Are you sure?"

"Yes, Charlie, I want you to have it."

Adam takes a deep breath and turns to look at Charlie. He asks, "Do you think God is angry with me?"

Charlie finds the question rather odd and hesitates before answering. "No. Why would you think that? Believe me, God knows how devoted you are."

"I think he's angry with me."

"Why would you think that?"

Adam doesn't know how to tell Charlie, so he sits on the edge of the bed, takes a deep breath, and thinks of a lie. "Because this morning when I awoke, I felt as if something was missing. I used to wake to a joyful feeling. Now I have a void. If there was ever a moment in my life when I felt trapped, I think it would be today. I had a horrible dream last night, and it kept me awake for hours. It's the same kind of dream I've been having for weeks now. I'm sick of these nightmares. I have no idea what they mean. I feel like an outcast in a world full of sheep. I don't belong here. I need the Lord to heal me from my pain. I wish I was anywhere far from here. The constant reminder of my obligation frightens me. How am I to face the challenges that others expect me to fail?"

"And you think that running away is the answer?"

"Yes. If I leave now, the headmaster won't preach to me."

"Then I suggest that you fill that void. Maybe you can find work that fulfills the gospel in another way."

"If God is still with me," says Adam with a blank expression.

"I don't think he has left your side," says Charlie. "You need to have a bit more faith. Remember that God will always be with you. All you have to do is believe."

"Thank you, Charlie. Somehow your words inspire me. It's getting late, so I'd better get going. I want to leave before anyone notices I'm gone."

Charlie is saddened and tries to console Adam as he escorts him to the gate. "You know, Adam, every now and then we have to make difficult choices. Sometimes we lose ourselves, and sometimes we discover who we really are. Life is full of many roads, and it can be confusing at times, but you must never forget who you are, who you want to be, and who you will become. Those are questions you must ask yourself, and I hope you will not stray from the path and will continue your journey of enlightenment. Adam, you have a special gift. You just have to discover it."

"Thank you, Charlie. I shall never forget you."

"Go now, my friend, and leave in peace," Charlie says, smiling. "I promise you, I won't say a word. Just remember that God is always with you, and never give up hope, no matter what. Obstacles may come your way, but there is a solution to every problem. You just have to believe."

"What will I do if I fail again?" Adam asks. "What will become of me?"

"That is a question I cannot answer," says Charlie, looking sadly at Adam.

"I feel so lost and confused," says Adam. "I don't even know where the nearest town is."

"See that road? Take it and continue north. I have heard of a beautiful town up that way, maybe half a day's walk. If you leave now, you could get there before evening. Go, and may God bless you on your journey."

Adam gives Charlie a farewell hug. "Thank you, Charlie. Thank you for being a great friend."

"I'm going to miss you."

Without looking back, Adam takes a deep breath and begins to walk north. Charlie stands out by the gate and watches Adam until he is out of sight.

As he walks, Adam talks quietly to himself. "I haven't set foot outside the monastery for many years, and I do not know where I am going. All I know is that I have to leave, because I am not worthy to fulfill the promise I made to my mother and to God. I have a long walk ahead of me, and I must go forth and see if I can begin a new life in that town. It will be hard, since I have no money and no family nearby, but I have my faith, and I know God will not abandon me."

When he grows tired, Adam stops and looks around. The road seems to never end. This heat is wearing him out. He decides to sit in the shade under a tree by the road. He notices a dark cloth bag near another tree and decides to take a look.

It seems to be a sack of some sort. Curious about the contents, he wonders if he should open it. Part of him says to do it, but something else tells him not to. He is unsure of what he should do. The bag is tied tight, and whatever is inside is pretty heavy. He thinks there can be no harm in opening the bag.

Adam looks around to make sure he's alone. He unties the bag and discovers that it is filled with money. He wonders who left it there. Could it be a gift from God? Is God helping Adam, or has someone lost this money? He doesn't think anyone would have lost this. It must be a gift. He believes that God is looking out for him. Adam looks to the sky and yells, "Thank you, Lord! Thank you for your generosity!"

Adam puts the sack of money into his backpack and continues walking north. The town shouldn't be far ahead.

Charlie mentioned that the town is immaculate, full of old statues, and that the people in the city are generous and have warm hearts. Strangers are welcomed. That sounds fine to Adam. He hopes that this is the same town Charlie described.

Adam continues walking until he sees something in the distance. "I don't believe it," he says aloud. "I must be near the town, but I haven't heard of a dragon being there. Is that a statue? Maybe it's the town mascot. But there are two of them, one on either side of the entrance. And there's even a welcome sign posted. 'Welcome to Rennis.' Now, that sounds comforting."

Adam stands outside the town and is amazed. The unexpected beauty of its buildings takes his breath away. He wonders how long it took to build such divine art.

Chapter 4

THE TOWN: 10:00 A.M.

Adam walks into the town and meets a stranger who is sitting by the entrance.

"Hello and welcome to Rennis."

"Thank you," Adam says, smiling. "This place looks amazing. Can you help me? I'm new to this town, and I need a place to stay during my visit. Could you point me to a hotel?"

"Sure, stranger, I can help accommodate you. In fact, I can give you a tour of the town, if you like."

"That would be great! Tell me, what's your name?"

"My name is Demantos."

Having never heard the name before, Adam frowns, but he extends his hand and introduces himself. "My name is Adam."

Demantos sees Adam's hand extended and gives it a tight squeeze. "Let me show you the town inn. Follow me, right this way."

Adam thinks to himself that Demantos is an odd name, but the man is extremely good-looking and very young. He has a pale complexion and long, dark hair. He is slender and fit. A man like that can get far in life, using his beauty to get into places. This makes Adam mad. He doesn't think he's bad-looking himself, but this man is exceptional.

The buildings in this town are amazing. They look old, maybe built during the Victorian period.

"Come in, Adam," says Demantos. "This is our town's inn, and as you can see, we take pride in our community. We work very hard to keep the town in perfect condition. Everything you see is original—no replicas whatsoever—and it's been this way for many generations. I hope you will enjoy your stay here with us in Rennis."

"Demantos, is there any way you can stay and be my guide?" Adam asks.

Demantos smiles and nods. "Of course! I mentioned that I could give you a tour of the town. I figured you wanted to rest first."

"No," says Adam happily, "I'm too excited to rest. There's so much to see, and I would like to get started as soon as possible."

"Let's just get you checked in first."

Adam looks nervously at a large man approaching the service desk. "Hello, Mason," Demantos says to him. "This is Adam. He would like a room for the night."

"Just one night?" asks Mason.

Demantos turns to Adam. "I'm sorry, how long were you planning on staying?" Adam, uncertain of his plans, mumbles, "A few weeks, I suppose."

"Well, then," says Mason, "that's better for you. We have weekly specials, and I think I have just the room to accommodate you. Just sign the registry. You can pay a deposit now and the rest when you leave."

Remembering the money he found, Adam smiles. "How much is it?"

"It will cost you about three hundred and thirty-three dollars, which includes the deposit."

"Just give me a second," says Adam.

"Is it going to be cash or credit?" asks Mason.

"Cash," Adam says, nervously thinking about the money he is carrying with him. Does he dare open the bag in front of them? Maybe he can use the restroom and take the money out there. "I'm sorry," he says to Mason. "Do you have a restroom?"

"It's down the hall to the right."

"I'll just be a minute," says Adam, smiling, and he rushes to the restroom. He just can't afford to let anyone see the money. He doesn't want to get robbed. He will only take out what he needs and then make his way back to the service desk. He can't trust anyone, and he can't afford to make any mistakes. The last thing he needs is for people to take advantage of him. He doesn't want to get tricked into anything, so he decides to take precautions in what he says and does. Adam hurries back to the front desk and notices that Demantos and Mason are laughing.

"I'm sorry about that. I had a long walk."

"You don't need to explain," says Mason.

"Here you are—three hundred and thirty-three dollars." Adam hands Mason the money for the room.

"Do you have any luggage?" asks Mason.

"No," Adam says hastily. "This is all I have."

Mason turns his back to him and grabs a room key. "Here you go. Room key two hundred and sixty-six."

"Thank you, and here's a little something for you." Adam gives Mason a two hundred-dollar tip. Mason looks at it and thanks Adam.

Adam addressed Demantos. "I'll just be a few minutes."

"Take your time," says Demantos, as he watches Adam run up the staircase.

"He seems a bit nervous," says Mason. "Kind of odd that he returned with the money in his hands."

"You shouldn't worry about him," says Demantos. "You know very well that strangers come and go. This one is no different."

"I don't know. I have my suspicions. He gave me a big tip."

"You shouldn't suspect everyone you meet. He's only been in town a few minutes, and already you're judging him."

Mason looks upstairs. Adam is making his way back downstairs, and it appears he has heard part of their conversation.

"What's going on?" Adam asks.

"What do you mean?" questions Demantos.

Concerned, Adam tells a lie. "I think I might be leaving tonight."

"But I was just telling Mason that you really need more time to enjoy the splendor of this town. You can't see it all in one day."

Mason sees Demantos's frown and agrees with him. "Yes, yes, it's true. It takes time to see every artifact and sight that this town has to offer. I suggest you begin by meeting more people. Maybe they can point out some of our tourist attractions to you."

"That sounds like a great idea," says Adam. "Do you think you can introduce me to some of your friends?"

Demantos turns and looks angrily at Mason. Then he slowly looks at Adam. Glancing at his watch, he sees that it is after 12:00 p.m., and he smiles at Adam. "I guess I could. Are you ready?"

Adam looks at Mason with a happy expression. "I shall return later this evening."

As they leave the service desk, Demantos looks back and stares at Mason with an evil smile. Mason sees Demantos looking directly at him and turns away. Demantos and Adam make their way to the front doors.

"Adam," says Demantos, "this town is home to many different cultures, but each individual adds his or her own uniqueness to the town, thus generating a unity of understanding and learning. So please don't be hasty and judge individuals. There's more to a person than his appearance. You must remember to keep an open mind." Crossing the street, Demantos sees the local pub and decides to take Adam there first. "I think we shall begin here at the pub." Demantos opens the door to the pub, and Adam's eyes light up with excitement.

"Demantos, is that you?" asks a female voice.

Adam says to himself, Who is she? I have never seen such a beautiful lady. She is a vision and takes my breath away. I have never felt feelings like this before.

"It's so kind of you to join us today," says the woman. "Who's your friend?"

Seeing Adam's smile, Demantos introduces him to her. "Jaden, this is Adam. He's visiting our town."

Adam grabs Jaden's hand and bestows a kiss on it. "A pleasure, my lady."

Jaden smiles at Adam as he releases her hand. She turns away from Adam and continues to have a conversation with Demantos. Feeling angry, Adam begins talking to himself. "Why is this beautiful creature talking to him and not to me? I'm the stranger in this town. She should be trying to meet me and forget him. The more I look at her, the more I want her. I have to have her, and no one is going to stop me—not even Demantos. I have never had any previous relationships with women, but for some strange reason I desire to have her at any cost, and it angers me that she doesn't look my way."

Demantos, seeing the vague expression on Adam's face, turns to call him. "Are you all right?"

Lost in thought, Adam quickly turns to see who is calling him. "What?" Adam says.

"I was asking Jaden if she could join us in showing you the town," Demantos says.

Hearing Jaden's name, Adam smiles and agrees. "That would be great. You don't mind?" he asks as he looks at her.

"No, not at all," says Jaden. "I'd do anything for Demantos."

Adam feels angry and bites his lip.

"I bet you're hungry," says Demantos. "Let me order you something to eat. Is there anything that you particularly like?"

"No," Adam says angrily.

"Then I shall order you our town's signature dish. I'm sure it will be to your liking. If you'll excuse me, I'll go place the order."

Adam waits for Demantos to leave and then turns to looks at Jaden with a smile. "Tell me, Jaden, what's a beautiful girl doing in a town like this?"

Jaden sees the smile on Adam's face and frowns. "Just trying to survive."

"Do you have a profession?" Adam asks nervously.

Jaden looks away and hesitates in her response. "I guess you could call it a profession."

"What is it that you do?" asks Adam.

"I'm a female caller."

Adam does not know what that is, and he questions Jaden about it.

Jaden is surprised and explains her job description to him. "I accompany men on their outings to private parties and gatheringsfor a price."

"Would you care to join me this evening?" asks Adam.

"That would depend on whether or not you can afford me."

Adam is puzzled. He looks down and fails to see that Demantos has returned and is standing near him. "Afford you? How much do you charge?"

Demantos interrupts him. "Adam, your meal is ready."

Adam mumbles angrily to himself. "I was so close, but he just had to interrupt." Adam takes a seat on a nearby stool and continues looking at Jaden. "Aren't you two going to join me?"

"No," says Demantos. "I only ordered for you."

"I don't want to eat alone," Adam says hesitantly.

"I was just joking," says Demantos. "Our plates are almost ready. I just wanted you to try it first."

"You don't mind that I eat before you two?" asks Adam.

Adam sees a change of expression on Jaden's face as she turns to look at more people who are entering the pub. "If you'll excuse me," she says, "I see someone that I must say hello to. I'll be back in a bit."

"Take your time," says Demantos.

Adam watches Jaden's every move and is sad when he sees her give a hug to someone else. The aroma of the food overwhelms him as he stirs the soup. "This looks tasty," he says. "What is it?"

"Lamb, of course," says Demantos.

"Lamb soup? I don't think I've ever eaten lamb before."

"Try it. I'm sure you'll like it. Trust me; it's very tasty."

Adam takes one bite and feels the meat melting in his mouth. He is amazed at how good it is. He consumes the entire bowl within minutes.

Demantos seems amazed at Adam's rapid consumption of the soup. "Would you care for more?" he asks.

"You are right," says Adam. "This is good. I can't believe how great it is, and yes, I'd like another bowl."

"Adam, you're welcome to have as much as you like, and don't worry about the check."

"Are you sure? I can afford it. I have lots of money."

"Sure I'm sure," says Demantos with a grin. "It's on me, so eat all you want."

Adam continues to indulge in the lamb soup and then begins drinking wine. Without realizing it, Adam consumes six bowls and still feels hungry. He continues to eat and eat without remorse. Jaden appears to be disgusted by Adam's consumption and walks over to get a closer look at his eating habits. Hearing her voice, Adam stops eating and looks directly at her as she walks right past him.

"Do you think you've had enough, or do you still want more?" asks Demantos.

Looking up at Demantos, Adam thinks about Jaden and decides to stop eating. "I think I will wait a bit." Adam looks around for Jaden, sees her stepping outside, and quickly changes his mind. "Well, on second thought, I'm sure I can eat a bit more."

"Are you sure?" asks Demantos, surprised.

"Yes, I'm sure. It's really good, and I can't seem to get my fill."

"You are aware that you have already eaten six bowls of the soup."

"A soup this tasty doesn't deserve to be rationed. You said I could have all I want, and I want more. It's just that damn good."

"I think you've had enough. You really shouldn't overeat."

"I don't care about overeating," says Adam. "I love this soup. It's my body, and if I want to continue, I will."

Adam hears the door open and checks his watch. It's now 5:00 p.m. Jaden has come back inside the pub. Adam begins talking to himself. She is the one person he craves, and he feel that he will never be fulfilled until he has her. Seeing her having conversation with others makes him angry. He wonders why she isn't talking to him, as he is the one who longs to have her.

Returning with another bowl of soup, Demantos sees Adam staring at Jaden. "What's wrong?" Demantos asks him. "Wait. I think I know."

Adam interrupts Demantos to ask about Jaden's company. "Who's she talking to?"

Demantos turns and looks at Jaden. "Adam," he says, "Jaden is not a normal girl. She has needs and is probably looking for her next client."

"Client?" says Adam.

"Yes, Adam, she's a call girl."

"I could be her next client."

"You?" says Demantos, laughing. "I don't think you're her type."

Adam feels frustrated and mumbles, "But if she needs the money, looks wouldn't matter."

"Adam, don't upset yourself. I meant no disrespect. Have you asked her?"

"I tried, but she won't even talk to me."

"Don't tell me you like her."

"I do," says Adam in a desperate voice. "I crave her. I have to have her."

"I can talk to her if you want."

Adam does not want to hear Demantos's suggestion. "No! I would rather do it my way. All I need to do is get her attention somehow."

"Listen to me. I can call her for you."

Adam anxiously agrees. "All right, then, go call her."

Demantos takes leave of him and walks up to Jaden. Unsure of himself, Adam talks to himself. "I wonder what he's telling her. It must be something good, because she's smiling. I must find a way to speak to her away from him and everyone else. I just can't believe that everyone here seems to respect Demantos. Damn! Why can't I be that way? If I were him, I bet she would want me. I hate him and his good looks. Look at him. He's friendly, funny, handsome, and interesting. Me, I'm just no one."

Adam puts his head down on the table to fantasize about Jaden.

"Adam," Demantos says, "she's waiting. Go speak with her."

"What?"

"She's waiting," says Demantos.

Adam feels nervous. He doesn't know what to say. What should he tell her? The closer he gets, the more his heart is pounding. "Jaden," he says to her, "could I please speak with you?"

"What is it?" she asks.

"There's something I want to ask you," says Adam nervously.

"I'm listening," says Jaden, looking around.

"We didn't get a chance to finish our conversation. Would like you to join me tonight? Money is no object."

"I don't know," says Jaden doubtfully. "I have other clients."

"I'm sure you can see them anytime. I'm not going to be here in town very long, and you really have nothing to lose. I'm offering you anything you want in exchange for one night."

"You tempt me like the Devil. Are you trying to make a deal?" says Jaden sarcastically.

Adam makes a fist and yells, "No, I'm better than the Devil. I can offer you more than anyone ever could."

"Adam, what about—"

"I'm even better than him," Adam interrupts, not wanting Jaden to finish her sentence. "Trust me."

"But you didn't let me finish my sentence," says Jaden angrily.

"It doesn't matter," says Adam, smiling. "I'm still the best."

"If you say so. I'll give you a chance to prove yourself. I just need to tell Demantos."

"Why? You don't need to tell him anything," says Adam. "Come on. Let's just go."

"He needs to know. I'll be back in a minute. I have to tell Demantos."

Adam feels angry and mumbles to himself as he watches Jaden tell Demantos. Every time she looks at Demantos, Adam feels angry. He doesn't think it's jealousy, but what else could it be?

He wonders how he can express to her what he is feeling without her pushing him away. There must be something between them. He has never had this kind of feeling for any human—especially a woman. How is this possible? Just the touch of her hand gets him excited, but how is he to convince her that he's not a bad guy? Maybe he should buy her something to show his gratitude.

Adam keeps a close eye on Demantos and begins to smile when he sees Jaden approaching.

"Let's go," says Jaden.

Adam grabs Jaden by the arm and questions her. "Did he say anything?"

"No," says Jaden hesitantly. "Not really. He just said to be careful because you're a stranger. So, where are we going?"

"I figured we could go to my hotel and see what happens from there."

"I thought you wanted a tour of the town."

"That isn't necessary. We can go tomorrow or the next day or the day after that. I plan on staying here awhile."

Staring at her, Adam begins to reach out to her. Jaden sees this and takes a step back.

"I am sorry," Adam says. "You're very beautiful, and I have never seen such beauty before. I have spent most of my life secluded from people. Sometimes I forget my manners. Please forgive me."

"At least let me show you this old artifact we have in the town," says Jaden. "It's really old, and you might find it fascinating."

"Very well," says Adam, feeling excited. "Show me the artifact."

Adam and Jaden leave the pub and begin to walk up the middle of the street. From a distance, Adams sees a glass case.

Demantos steps outside the pub and watches Jaden and Adam. Slowly another man with long, dark hair joins him outside.

"Who is that with Jaden?" the man asks.

"His name is Adam."

"Adam?"

"Pay no attention to him," says Demantos. "He just arrived not too long ago, and he seems very interested in Jaden."

"He'd better watch himself. He has no idea who he's with."

"You're right. He doesn't. But don't worry about it. He is just another lost soul trying to find his way."

"I think he came to the wrong town."

Demantos is getting angry and yells at the man. "He mustn't be harmed, so keep your distance!"

"Adam, look at this," says Jaden.

"What is it?"

"This is part of our town history. Everything that has ever happened in our town is in this book."

Adam gets closer to the glass case and leans over to look at it. "I don't see what is so special about that book. It looks plain. No designs on the cover or anything. It's just a plain, black book. I don't see how this could hold the town's history."

Jaden looks at Adam with an angry expression. "Adam, you don't seem to understand. To the naked eye, it looks plain, but believe me, this book is truly beautiful, and it is covered in gold lettering."

"You're pulling my leg," Adam says. "I don't see anything. Maybe if we were to take the glass case apart, I could see it."

"No!" yells Jaden. "You can't take it apart. It's forbidden! I only wanted to show it to you because it is important to me. I treasure every word in that book. It holds a lot of history. That is why it is incased."

"Then why can't I see anything?"

"Because you have to belong to the town. Outsiders rarely even get a glance at it."

"Then I want to be part of your town!" shouts Adam. "That way I can see the book, but more importantly I can see you."

Down the street, Demantos's eyes widen with excitement when he hears Adam yell.

"Ow!" Adam cries out as he caresses the glass case.

"What is it?" asks Jaden.

"I think I just cut my finger on the glass."

"That's impossible. The glass isn't sharp."

"Well, something pricked me."

"Come, Adam, let's go," Jaden says. "Where to now? What else would you like to see?"

Adam looks at his finger and sees his blood drip onto the glass case. "Maybe we should go to the hotel to clean my finger," he says.

"Whatever you want," says Jaden.

Adam smiles. He feels more confident in himself. He has Jaden by the arm, and they're leaving this wretched area of town and going to his hotel room, where he believes he will enjoy her.

"Why the rush?" asks Jaden.

"I want to hurry because it's cold outside, and a lovely lady like yourself deserves to be in the comfort of warmth."

Arriving at the hotel, Adam looks at the clock on the wall and sees that it's 8:00 p.m. He keeps a lookout for Mason, who is helping another customer at the moment and doesn't notice Adam rushing right by him with Jaden.

"Here we are," says Adam happily.

Jaden looks a bit nervous as she smiles and takes a look around the hotel room.

"I want you," says Adam.

"What?"

"I want you."

"What about your finger?" asks Jaden.

Impatient, Adam walks up to Jaden and begins kissing every part of her body before laying her on the bed. He then begins to undress her and himself. Jaden's hand brushes up against his organ, and Adam feels it come to life. Slowly he begins making love to her.

When daylight enters the room, Adam is excited to watch Jaden as she awakes. "My darling, awaken," he whispers in her ear. "It's morning. I want take you out for breakfast."

"I'm not hungry," Jaden says. "What time is it?"

Without saying a word, Adam begins to think about Demantos and his connections in this town. "Wait here, my love," he says, kissing Jaden on the forehead. "I'll be back in a few hours. I just need to look for someone."

"Where are you going?" asks Jaden.

"Don't worry. I'll be right back. Just promise me that you'll still be here."

"Adam, I can't promise anything," says Jaden sadly, looking at the time on the wall clock.

Adam looks at the clock and realizes that it is now 9:15 a.m. I'd better hurry, he thinks. I have to find him. Thinking for a minute, Adam remembers the pub. Demantos may be there. Adam walks by the entrance to the town and hears Demantos calling out to him.

"You're up early, Adam."

"I need to talk to you," Adam says.

"Is something wrong?" asks Demantos as he approaches.

"No, not really," says Adam.

"Did something go wrong with Jaden?"

"No, that's not it." Adam takes a step back. "I need to make more money. I believe it's the only way she'll stay with me. She could live a life of luxury and never have to work again."

Demantos looks at Adam and answers quickly. "You can have all the money you need."

"I don't want to lose her," says Adam sadly.

"Today is Sunday, a day made for rest," says Demantos.

"I don't care what day it is!" yells Adam, waving his arms in the air.

"Are you sure?"

"Of course I am," yells Adam. "This day is like any other. There's no special reason to rest. I need money! What should I do?"

"You seem desperate. Was the night with her that good?"

"Yes!" Adam says with excitement. "It was the best experience of my life and the happiest moment ever. Don't you understand that I can't let her go? What do I need in order to survive here?"

"Adam, there are many people who have given up everything and everyone they love in order to live here. They have had their desires fulfilled and find themselves here afterward."

"I want to be one of them," Adam says angrily. "I want to be here so I can be near her."

"Do you understand what I'm saying?" asks Demantos.

Angry, Adam moves closer to Demantos and says, "I want this! I want her!"

Demantos, doubting Adam, questions his reason. "Is she the only reason?"

"She's one of the reasons," Adam says, smiling. "I also love the lamb soup, and it bothers me that I feel this way for her. I told her I'm better than anyone else. I believe I proved that last night." Adam looks directly into Demantos's eyes and tells him, "I hate it when I don't get what I want, and I want her, and it pisses me off." Adam glares at Demantos. "I know she likes you. I can see it."

"And that bothers you?" Demantos asks, looking at his watch.

"Yes! Everyone likes you, and I wish I was you!"

"I highly doubt that you want what I have, believe me. But tell me: how do you feel about religion?"

"Religion!" yells Adam. "Why are you asking me this? I don't care about religion. What does religion have to do with what I feel? Right now, I don't feel very religious. In fact, I'm beginning to have doubts about religion. I don't need sermons or preaching from you or anyone else. That's the last thing on my mind."

"I'm sorry I mentioned it," says Demantos, smiling. "Don't get angry. Listen, I have to go somewhere, but I'll be back shortly."

"I'm going to return to the hotel and check on Jaden," says Adam. "I'll meet you back here in a few minutes."

Chapter 5

SINS REVEALED: THE CONFRONTATION

Adam returns to the hotel and frantically begins searching for Jaden. Unable to find her, Adam is suspicions of Demantos and decides to go look for him. Leaving the hotel, Adam sees Demantos sitting on a rock by the town entrance.

"Where is she?" Adam yells as he confronts Demantos and grabs him by the shirt.

"Temper, temper. I haven't seen her."

"You lie! Tell me where she is. I know you've seen her."

"Tell me, Adam: what would you do if I could make her yours?"

Adam puts his guard down and takes a step back to think about the question. "Anything, I suppose," he says.

"Are you aware of everything you have done in the past twenty-four hours?" asks Demantos, his eyes wide.

"I don't have time for your riddles. I have to find her!" yells Adam, turning his back on Demantos.

"And what will you do after you find her?"

"That's none of your business!"

Curious, Demantos gets off the rock, stands behind Adam, and whispers into his ear. "Would you die for her?"

"Yes," Adam says slowly.

Liking the response to his question, Demantos asks other questions. "Would you kill for her?"

"Yes!"

"Would you lie for her?"

"Yes," says Adam angrily. "She is my temple."

"Would you devote your life to her?"

"Yes, I would sell my soul just to have her," Adam says. "Don't you understand? I have to be with her!"

Demantos, surprised by this answer, asks Adam, "What did you say?"

"You heard me."

Demantos looks to the sky and smiles. "I'm sure I did, but did he?"

"He who?"

"I think you should say it a bit louder," says Demantos as he turns to face Adam.

"Yes, I would sell my soul just to have her!"

Adam is frightened by a sudden change of weather and begins to question Demantos. "What's going on? Why is it getting dark? Is there some kind of eclipse?"

"No, Adam," says Demantos with an evil grin.

"Then what's happening? Tell me!" Adam yells. "Where's Jaden?"

Demantos begins walking around Adam in circles. "Do you really want to know where she is? Pay close attention, Adam. Why don't you ask Jaden yourself?"

"What?" asks Adam.

Demantos sees the frightened look in Adam's eyes and laughs. "Look to your left, Adam. What do you see?"

"Jaden!" Adam screams. "You nailed her to a cross, you son of a bitch!" Adam shoves Demantos. "Get her down!"

"If you want to save her, you will have to go through me!" Demantos yells.

"I don't want to fight you. Let her go!"

Demantos sees the frustration in Adam's face and turns to face him with a smile. "Oh, I'll let her down—for a price, that is. You said you would do anything for her, and now is your chance."

Adam is frightened and doesn't know what to say. He runs up to the cross where Jaden has been crucified and looks at the blood dripping from her arms and feet. "Jaden! Answer me!" Adam cries.

"Do you really think she can hear you?" asks Demantos. "The girl is out cold, I'm afraid."

Adam extends his hand to touch Jaden's feet. "Fine. What must I do?"

"You have already done it," says Demantos, grinning.

"Done what? What are you talking about?"

"You see, Adam, things aren't always what they appear to be, and thanks to you, I was able to demonstrate something very important."

Adam sees the gleam in Demantos's eyes and is frightened. "And what's that?" he asks.

Demantos slowly walks over to Adam and looks up at Jaden. "Would you really die for her?"

Adam, saddened at the thought of losing Jaden, sheds a tear. "Yes," he says.

"Adam, what if I were to tell you that Jaden isn't who you think she is?"

"What are you talking about?"

Demantos raises his hand and points at Jaden. "Adam, you deserve to know the truth. Look at me. What do you see?"

Adam is not sure of the question and turns to look at Demantos. "I see you."

"Adam, why did you stray from the path? Why did you abandon the monastery?"

Adam is surprised by the question and turns his back on Demantos. "The monastery? How could you know about that?"

Demantos moves to stand in front of Adam and smiles. "I know everything, Adam. I know you grew up feeling unfulfilled.

34

I know your secret. In fact, are you familiar with the seven deadly sins?"

"Yes," Adam says slowly, swallowing.

"Tell me what they are," says Demantos in a demanding voice.

Adam trembles as he speaks. "Pride, envy, gluttony, lust, anger, greed, and sloth." Looking down, Adam begins to worry.

"Very good, Adam," says Demantos with a smile. "Now, tell me how many you have committed."

"What? None! I've committed none!"

"Adam, you need not lie. You are aware that you have committed all seven deadly sins."

"What's really going on here?"

"Adam, do you have any idea who I really am?"

Frightened, Adam closes his eyes. "No, and I'm beginning to worry."

"It's like I said. I know everything about you. You can't keep secrets from me, and out of thousands and thousands of humans, I chose you."

"Why me?" asks Adam.

"Because, Adam, I needed to prove a point about humans and their defiance toward their beliefs. I know you were an ordained servant of God, and you failed to commit to your promises and obligations."

"Who are you?" asks Adam angrily.

"I have many names. You said you would sell your soul, and I just happen to be in the market for a new one."

Adam cries out, "Lucifer! No, it can't be! This is a bad dream, and I'm still asleep!"

"I assure you that this is no dream. I am very real, and despite the outcome, you now belong to me."

"No! God, heavenly Father, banish this demon from my sight!"

Lucifer laughs and nods his head. "Yell, cry, and call out to him, but there is just one problem. It's been over twenty-four hours since this test started, and during that time you

35

gave no mention or appraisal of God, though you had many opportunities to do so. In fact, I do believe that you were stating that you were even better than he is, and that too is a sin. Your time is up."

Adam angrily looks Lucifer in the eyes. "I don't know how you did it. You tricked me and Jaden."

"Tricked you? No, my dear boy, you did this on your own, and if you turn and look at Jaden, you will see that she's not even human." Frightened, Adam runs to look at Jaden and sees her turn into a demon. "No! God, where are you?"

"Didn't you hear a word I said? You're mine. Because of my promises, I cannot kill you, but I am going to place my mark on your flesh. Every day when you see it, you'll know that I own you. You belong to me, and I can wait for all eternity. When you die, God won't be there. *I* will be there, and I'm going to take you where you belong—to hell with me, and no amount of goodness will save you. I will be watching."

In denial, Adam yells, "This can't be happening to me! I don't believe you!" Lucifer walks up to Adam and touches his chest. "What are you doing to me? Let me go. Get away from me!"

"Remember, Adam, no amount of prayer will save you. No good deeds or sacrifices will ever lift my mark. You now belong to me!"

"No! You may have my body, but you can never take my soul!" Adam cries as he breaks free from Lucifer and begins to run.

"I already have!" Lucifer watches Adam run from the town. "Go! Run and hide, but believe me, I will always know where you are. You can never escape from me. Never!" He lowers his voice and smiles. "You have already lost, my dear boy, and now the waiting begins."

Chapter 6

SECOND ENCOUNTER: THE DISBELIEF

Lucifer smiles, not realizing that Michael has returned and witnessed him marking Adam's flesh with his demonic seal. Slowly Michael walks toward Lucifer.

Lucifer stops laughing when he senses that he is not alone. Standing still with his arms stretched before him, Lucifer begins creating a ball of fire. As Michael gets closer, he realizes that Lucifer might be on to him.

Lucifer releases the ball of fire at Michael. Michael sees the ball of flame coming toward him and instantly jumps out of the way. He looks directly at Lucifer, who is preparing to launch another ball of flame at him.

"Lucifer, I'm here on neutral grounds!" yells Michael. Lucifer, seeing Michael's expression, decides to hold back his ball of flame, and it disintegrates in his hands.

"You call this neutral ground, sneaking up on me?" Lucifer says. "I bet you were planning to attack me from behind." He walks toward Michael with a serious expression.

"I meant no disrespect. I only wanted to surprise you."

"Surprise me? Why? I find that impossible to believe. Tell me why you have come."

Michael, seeing that Lucifer is getting closer to him, decides to take a few steps back. "I'm here on business matters."

"What business matters?" asks Lucifer angrily. "We have nothing to discuss."

"You may not think so, but we do. You cheated."

"Cheated? How? When? I did nothing of the sort."

"Somehow you managed to manipulate the human named Adam and blind him from thinking on his own."

"I did no such thing," says Lucifer. "I followed the rules. It's not my fault that God hates losing."

"Losing?" Michael says. "No, you're mistaken. God never loses. In fact, right now, at this moment, he is working on a solution to this situation."

"You can't win, and I know this angers you, because now you're frantically trying to come up with some lame plan to stop me from claiming what is rightfully mine. But it won't work, because I have already won."

"You can keep telling yourself that, but we both know that this is far from being over, and believe me, you've already lost. It's only a matter of time before you come to realize it."

Lucifer pauses for a minute and looks around. Then he focuses his attention on Michael and smiles with an evil grin. "Michael, you seem to forget that I have the upper hand. I have left my mark on this human, and all I have left to do is wait, wait for his last breath before I can claim him."

"Remove your mark and give him a fair chance."

"No, I don't think I will. It is a reminder of what awaits him after death, so I can't."

Michael is angry and pleads, "Release him."

"Like I said—no."

"Very well, then. I tried to give you a fair chance, but because of your stubbornness, you have left me no choice."

"What are you talking about?" asks Lucifer.

Michael smiles. "Lucifer, do you really think I would come here unprepared for you, for this?"

"You don't frighten me, Michael, and I highly doubt that you have come prepared."

Michael studies Lucifer's movements. "Really? You doubt me? Well, just wait and see."

"You were always full of yourself," says Lucifer. "That's why no one ever shows devotion to you."

"You lie, and you know it. But it doesn't matter. God will win. You just wait and see."

Michael looks to his left and his right and then smiles. Seeing this, Lucifer takes a step back and begins creating ball of flame in his hand. In response, Michael nods his head, and two balls of light are released to strike Lucifer on either side. Lucifer launches his flame to Michael's right and left, hitting his targets—two angels, who are suddenly revealed and wounded.

Michael draws his sword and moves toward Lucifer. Lucifer smiles as he throws balls of flame at Michael. The two wounded angels create balls of light to launch at Lucifer. Michael gets close to Lucifer and swings his sword. Feeling the tip of the blade brush against him, Lucifer launches a ball of flame directly at Michael, which sends him flying backward against a tree. The two angels frantically send more balls of light at Lucifer, but they keep missing him. Michael rises from the ground and launches multiple balls of light at Lucifer. Lucifer is having a hard time diverting this intense attack, so he summons two demons to fight against the two angels.

Michael focuses his attention on Lucifer. "You can't win! Give it up!" he yells.

"Give up? Never! I shall win this!" Lucifer shouts.

Michael launches a ball of light that hits Lucifer directly. Lucifer feels the hit and yells, "Is that the best you can do?"

Michael charges Lucifer with his sword in hand. Lucifer sees the blade coming toward him, grabs the tip, and struggles to keep it from striking him. The demons, seeing that Lucifer is close to being stabbed by Michael's sword, begin launching balls of fire at Michael. The two angels send more balls of light at the demons. Michael falls back and summons his angels.

"This isn't over," Michael yells angrily. "We shall meet again." He ascends to the sky and takes flight.

Seeing that Michael is escaping, Lucifer sends more flame after him, but Michael dodges the attack. Lucifer takes flight to pursue him, continuing his onslaught. Michael turns back, a ball of light forming in his hands. The two manage to strike each other, and both fall toward the ground. Michael finds a way to slow himself, pulling himself up and spreading his wings. When he regains control, he resumes his attack on the still falling Lucifer. Feeling the pain of Michael's weapons, Lucifer tries to return fire as he falls, but Michael merely maneuvers aside and ascends higher into the sky.

Lucifer hits the ground hard and slowly rises to look up at the sky. He surveys the battle site and suddenly begins to laugh. When his demons approach him, he yells for them to leave him. The demons walk away and slowly disappear.

"This isn't over, Michael," Lucifer says quietly. "You may have won this round, but we shall fight again, and next time I shall triumph over you. There is no chance that I am ever going to remove my mark from this mortal." He examines his wounds and laughs again. "Just flesh wounds, nothing else. Michael, you need more practice."

As Lucifer looks around, he remembers Adam's departure. "I think I'll pay a visit to my human and watch him weep. That should bring me some sort of satisfaction after what just happened here."

Chapter 7

DENIAL: THE SADNESS

Adam stops running and begins walking toward a river. "Why do I find myself alone?" he asks aloud. "I keep calling out to you, but there's no answer. Am I being punished for leaving the monastery? How can you deny me the comfort I so desperately need? Why won't you answer? What am I going to do? You promised that if I would call upon you, you would redeem me and spare me. Where are you? Have I offended you? Did I bring you shame? Whatever I've done, you can't hold this against me."

Adam feels angry and begins to pace.

"I know you set me up. You were testing me, weren't you? And I failed. I failed you, and I failed the church, but most of all I failed myself. I was a fool. I let one sin turn into many. But how could it *not* happen? It had to be a setup, because Lucifer was there. No! I won't believe it. I won't believe that you, God Almighty, set me up. You know I tried to be a dedicated servant, wishing only to glorify you. I never meant to hurt you. I should have seen the signs. I should have questioned everything, but it all happened so fast. I had no time to react. And now that I think about it, I have to ask why you let it happen? I need answers. Where are you? You can't just let this happen and then forget me!"

Adam feels unsure of himself. He begins to deny everything and finally has an anxiety attack. "No, wait, this is a bad dream.

I'm still at the monastery. That has to be it. What if I close my eyes and tell myself to wake up? Wake up! Wake up! Why isn't it working? What did I do to deserve this? How is it that I feel so empty and abandoned? When I left the monastery, I was alone, but I felt fine, knowing you were with me. Now, for some strange reason, I feel betrayed. I know I shouldn't blame you, but I can't help the way I feel. I've lost so much and gained nothing. What happened to all the promises I was told you would fulfill? What happened to my faith? How can I believe in anything I was taught, if I have no proof that you are even listening to me? I'm starting to get angry, and I'm beginning to hate you. How can you forsake me?"

Adam walks to the river, kneels down, and begins to splash water on his face. Suddenly he yells, "Why am I still here?" but there is no answer.

Disappointed, Adam takes off his shirt, stands in the water, and splashes more and more water on himself. It isn't until he notices a mark on his chest that he decides to stop. Looking at himself, he goes into shock and denial.

"What's this? No, it can't be. This is just a drawing. I can wash it off."

Adam scrubs his chest until it turns red. He uses his fingernails to scratch at the skin until it begins to bleed.

"Why isn't this coming off?" he yells. "What did I do?" In his current state of mind, he doesn't realize that Lucifer has been watching him.

"What's the matter, Adam?" says Lucifer.

Adam recognizes the voice and quickly turns around. "Lucifer!"

"Scared, Adam? You should be."

Adam wades out of the river and looks directly at Lucifer. "What did you do to me?"

"What didn't I do?" says Lucifer, smiling. "I just provided you with everything you wanted."

"You tricked me," says Adam angrily.

"Perhaps you tricked yourself. You wanted it, remember? I simply guided you."

"Why? Why me?" Adam asks sadly.

"Don't upset yourself, Adam. You should feel fortunate. You helped me prove something, and for that reason, when your time comes, when you find yourself in death's hands, remember that I shall welcome you with open arms."

Adam moves toward Lucifer. "I want nothing from you!"

"Perhaps not, but I have nothing else to offer you. I have already given you everything you wanted, and furthermore, I have already claimed my prize."

Adam is confused. "Prize? What prize?"

Smiling, Lucifer responds. "You, Adam. I own you."

"What?"

"It's very simple. You see, after your miserable death, God isn't the one who will be waiting for you. He's not the one who will send angels to enlighten your path and comfort your passing. I will be there and no one else. I will be your personal escort and will take you where you belong—into hell with me for all eternity."

"What? That can't be true. I don't believe you."

"It's true, Adam. Believe me. I have no reason to lie to you."

Adam begins to weep. "So, no matter what I do, I'll still end up in hell with you?"

"Yes, but look at it this way. You already know where your soul is going, so you really don't have to worry."

"Then answer me this: who chose me?"

Lucifer looks at Adam and takes a deep breath. "*I* chose you."

Adam is astonished. "Why?"

"Because there was something about you that I found intriguing. You have a certain 'something.'"

"And what would that be?"

"You may not believe me, but you and I have something in common, and I am going to let you figure out what that is. But I will give you a hint. Your actions speak louder than words."

"This can't be happening to me," says Adam.

Lucifer looks down at his seal on Adam's chest and smiles. "Adam, you know you can always call upon me just by rubbing your chest and calling my name."

"I want nothing from you," Adam says angrily. "Believe me, I am going to find a way to remove this mark from my chest."

Lucifer gives Adam an approving look. "That's one reason I chose you, Adam. You're a fighter, and I love a good challenge. Go ahead. I'd love for you to prove me wrong."

"I do not fear you, Lucifer. It's not over until I say it's over. You may think you have me, but you don't own me yet."

"Adam, my dear boy, you're so arrogant," Lucifer says, moving closer to him. "You don't realize that once my seal has been placed upon mortal flesh it can never be removed, unless God and I come to an agreement on that particular soul—and that has yet to happen, because I have never removed my seal from anyone."

"Like I said, Lucifer, your words have no effect on me."

"Adam, I will be watching you very closely, so if I were you, I would forget this nonsense of self-redemption. The sooner you accept your fate, the sooner you can continue to live your worthless life. Embrace me, Adam. Accept this, and accept me."

"Never. I'll find a way, you'll see. I am going to have the last laugh."

"You are very foolish. Try all you like, but remember that I have already won. If not for the promises I had to make, we would be having this conversation in hell."

Lucifer is angry. He takes one last look at Adam and charges toward him. Adam is paralyzed with fear, but Lucifer disperses into the air and disappears. In shock, Adam stands alone and begins to breathe heavily.

"I can't believe what just happened," says Adam, crying. "How can God allow it? I have no idea what I am going to do." Adam looks at his chest and sees Lucifer's seal. "I have to hide this somehow. I can't afford to have anyone see this. I'm ashamed of myself. I should have known better."

Chapter 8

THE RETURN: CHARLIE

Adam is having difficulty absorbing what has happened, so he decides to take a walk.

"God," he says aloud, "I felt something on that day you left my side. How do I fill the emptiness that I now feel? How can I forget the sadness that now consumes me? Why does it hurt me so? Is it too late for me?"

Adam is filled with remorse and guilt. He stops walking, looks behind him, and sees the distance he's already walked. Although he is sad, his mouth forms a half smile as he looks down the road ahead of him.

"I have blamed you for everything," he tells God. "I have let this anger blind me to the point of self-destruction. I can't do this any longer. I should end my life right now and dwell in the hell that I created. Lucifer will be waiting for me. I can feel his presence. I don't want him to win, but I can't go on. What else is there?"

Adam places his hand on his chest. He slowly nods his head and smiles. Suddenly he moves his hand.

"Wait a minute!" Adam shouts. "The monastery! What if I go back and see Charlie? I'm sure he'll know what to do. I mustn't waste any time. I have to find a way to save myself. I can't go to hell. I can't let Lucifer win. I must stop him at all costs."

Adam clenches his fists and looks at the ground. "Do you hear me? I shall find a way to stop you. You may have my body, but I will find a way to take back my soul. This isn't over. I will win back my freedom, with or without the help of God. The only sin I committed was in destroying my own soul."

Adam looks to the sky and shouts, "God, you had a big part in this. You could have stopped it, but you were too busy to save me, and because of your betrayal I have to fight a battle to save myself. If only you had been there for me in the beginning, this would not have happened to me."

As Adam continues to walk down the road, he realizes that he is getting closer to the monastery. He walks faster and faster as he talks to God.

"What I did and what I felt at the monastery should not be held against me. It gives you no right to judge me before my time. You created me his way. Wasn't it you who took me there to begin with? You gave my mom the idea. You knew this was going to happen to me. You had it all planed out. After all, you know everything before it happens." Adam continues walking until he reaches the monastery. Standing outside the gate, he can see Charlie in the distance.

"Charlie!" he yells.

Charlie recognizes Adam's voice and hurries to the gate. "Adam, what are you doing here? I thought you would be in the next town by now. They're looking for you, you know." Seeing Adam's sadness, Charlie unlocks the gate, and steps outside to talk with him.

"I need your help," Adam says. "Something terrible has happened to me. What I have to tell you is serious." He hesitates for a moment and looks around before continuing. "I'm kind of embarrassed and ashamed to tell you, but—"

"What is it, Adam? You can tell me."

Adam wants to be out of sight of all the other monastery residents. He looks around and sees a bench hidden behind some bushes and moves to sit there. "Charlie, there's something I have to show you, but I'm afraid you won't believe me even if I do."

Charlie joins Adam on the bench with a hesitant smile.

Adam is uncertain how to begin. He sighs deeply and smiles sadly at his friend. "Charlie, I've done a terrible thing, and God has forsaken me."

Charlie is not sure what Adam is trying to tell him, and he interrupts. "What are you talking about? God would never abandon his children."

"It's all so confusing," Adam says. "I don't know where to begin."

"Sometimes it's best to start at the beginning," says Charlie, looking worried.

Adam looks up at the sky and begins to weep.

"Adam, this must be really serious," says Charlie.

"Believe me, it is, but I have to tell you. After I ran away the other day, I felt I was alone, but I was happy at the same time. You had reminded me of God's love, and I felt everything would be fine. But I was wrong."

"I felt tired and went under a tree to rest a bit, and I found a sack full of money. I instantly thought that God had sent it to me. I was excited. I continued to walk and came across a town. I thought it was the town you had mentioned to me, but it wasn't." Adam feels nervous and stops to glance down at his chest.

Charlie anxiously presses Adam to continue. "Go on."

Adam looks up at Charlie and then lowers his head and continues. "The town was beautiful, just like the one you described, and I met someone there." Adam pauses for a second and clears his throat. "He helped me get a room in a hotel and introduced me to some of his friends."

"That doesn't sound too bad."

"Let me finish. It gets worse, far worse, believe me. Let's just say that according to this person and God, I have committed all forms of the deadly sins."

"Who is this person are you talking about?"

"Let's just say that I met him."

"Him who, Adam? Tell me."

"Lucifer, Charlie. I met Lucifer."

Charlie frowns. "I don't believe you."

"I knew you wouldn't, but believe me, my guide and friend turned out to be Lucifer."

"I am having a hard time believing you." Charlie looks anxiously at Adam as he slowly begins to raise his shirt.

"I have something to show you," Adam says. "Look!"

Charlie looks in amazement and wonder. "What is it? What happened to you? What are all those marks on your chest?"

"I've been marked," says Adam sadly.

"Marked?"

"I have Lucifer's seal on my chest, and there's no way to remove it."

Charlie is curious and begins to extend his hand.

"No, Charlie, please. You can't touch it," says Adam, pulling his shirt back down.

"How did this happen?"

"I was tricked."

"Tricked? I don't see how that's possible."

Adam looks away and begins to cry. "Charlie, I was played for a fool. The whole time I was in that God-forsaken town, I was being tested, and I failed."

"Adam, what was the name of the town?"

"Rennis."

"I've never heard of a town called Rennis. In fact, I don't believe that town exists. Hmm . . . do you have a pen on you?"

Adam searches his pockets. "No, I don't. Why?"

"Doesn't matter. I'll write in the dirt with a twig." Charlie carves the name *Rennis* into the sand, while Adam watches patiently. "Oh my God! Adam, come here. Take a look at this."

"What is it? What did you find out?"

"Read this. What does it say?"

"*Rennis.* Why?"

"Now read it backward," says Charlie.

Adam moved closer and suddenly froze with understanding. "Sinner," he read aloud. "No, it can't be."

"It is, Adam. The town is called Sinner, not Rennis. You're right. You were tricked."

Adam takes a look at Charlie and then turns away. "Do you think I'm being punished?" he asks.

"Punished? No. Why would you think that?"

"Look at me. I'm marked, and God has abandoned me. What else am I supposed to think? I have lost everything, including my faith."

"What are you saying? You know it's blasphemy to blame God. You brought this upon yourself by running away. God had nothing to do with it."

Adam stares at the crucifix in the garden. "You're right. I have no one to blame but myself."

"Listen to me," says Charlie. "Things happen for a reason. There's is no way that God would set you up. You're a man of the cloth, and I think God would look out for his own."

"As much as I would like to believe you, I can't. God has forsaken me."

"Adam, don't say such a thing. Remember your oath to the church."

"My oath? What good did it do me when I was left alone? Where was he when all this was happening to me?"

"I can understand your hurt, but keep in mind that you're not alone."

"I'm sorry, Charlie. I guess I let my anger get the best of me, but you have to understand that this is something I never thought would happen."

"You mentioned that you met a friend," Charlie says.

"Yes, and I made love to a girl who was really a demon."

"What? But you're a man of the cloth. No wonder all this has happened. You broke a carnal rule. How could you?"

"It wasn't me, believe me," Adam says in a sad voice. "I was tricked somehow. Help me, Charlie, please! I need you."

"Adam, there is only so much I can do."

Adam begins to cry and looks Charlie in the eyes. "I don't want to go hell," he says. "Lucifer will be waiting for me. I can't let him win."

"Maybe we should tell Father Leon."

"No! I don't want any of them to find out. This is my battle."

"What if you were to show me where this so-called town is? Maybe we can find clues there that can release you from his hold?"

"That's a great idea."

"First I have to get permission to leave the monastery," Charlie says. "Maybe I can tell them I'm homesick or something."

"I don't have much time to save my soul."

"Very well, but first let me get something from my room."

"I'll meet you at the front gate," says Adam. "Please hurry."

"Don't worry. We'll find a way to save your soul."

Adam waits for Charlie to walk into the monastery before departing from the table and making his way to the front gate. Slowly he looks to the sky and asks God, "Did I do something horrible to offend you?"

Suddenly Charlie is back at his side. "Are you ready?" he asks.

"That was fast."

"I only grabbed what I thought was necessary for the trip."

"Thank you so much for coming," Adam says. "I knew I could count on you. You truly are a great friend, and I can never repay you."

"Lead the way. Hopefully we'll be back before nightfall, and no one will know I left the monastery."

Adam and Charlie walk down the road toward the town. Feeling tired, Adam begins to slow down.

"What's wrong?" Charlie asks. "Why are you slowing down?"

"I don't know. I feel my chest getting heavy, and it's harder to breathe. I think I need to rest a bit."

Charlie looks at Adam with sadness and concern. "Maybe we should look for some shade under those trees."

Adam looks at the trees and remembers that this is the place where he found the money. "No, Charlie, let's not rest here."

"What happened here?"

Adam hesitates, not really wanting to explain.

"I think we should cross the road and retrace your footsteps."

"Do we have to? I'd rather not."

"How am I going to help you if you refuse to do what I tell you?"

Adam feels nervous, but he realizes that he has no choice but to listen to Charlie. Crossing the road, he is hesitant to go under the tree. He places his hand on his chest. "I found the money under this tree," he says.

"There's nothing here," says Charlie. "What did you do with it?"

"I left it in the town."

Charlie appears angry and shouts at Adam. "You left it in the town? Are you crazy?"

"Why are you yelling at me? It's only money."

"We could have used it at the monastery."

"But what if it was blood money?"

Charlie gives Adam an angry look. "How much further do we have to go?"

"It's only money," Adam insists, "and believe me, it didn't help me at all. In fact, I think it made matters worse."

Adam and Charlie continue walking down the road. Suddenly Adam stops and takes a deep breath.

"What's wrong?" asks Charlie.

"I feel something pulling me back."

"We must keep going. We're too far to turn back. Come on. We're almost there."

"What did you say?" Adam is feeling confused and doesn't press the matter.

"How much further is this town?" asks Charlie.

"It should be right up ahead. I remember that the first thing I saw was a statue of a dragon."

"A dragon?"

Adam and Charlie continue to walk. Adam feels tired and stops for a minute to look around.

"What's wrong?" Charlie asks.

"We should have found the town by now," Adam says. "I don't remember it being this far from the money."

"Maybe you were just too excited to notice how far the town really was."

"No, something's not right. We should have found the town by now."

"Tell me what the town looked like."

"Well, it was beautiful and perfect, full of old statues and carvings. Everything in the town was authentic, and they even had an old book encased in glass. The people were kind. It was great little town. Rennis—how splendid it was." As Adam continues to talk about the town, buildings slowly begin to appear. "What's going on?" he asks.

"It looks like the town is revealing itself."

"That's impossible. There's no way that could happen." Slowly Adam looks around. Soon he is standing in the middle of the town, right in front of the displayed book. "How can this be possible? Are you seeing this? Charlie, where are you?"

Adam looks around for Charlie and continues to call his name. He walks to the entrance of the town and sees Charlie standing there. "There you are! I was beginning to worry." He sees that Charlie's back is turned toward him. "Charlie, what's wrong?" he asks. "Why are you facing away from me?"

Chapter 9

THE FINAL BATTLE: DELIVERANCE

Slowly Charlie turns around. Adam looks into his eyes and takes a step back.

"I knew you would come back," says Charlie. "After all, you said you wanted to be part of this town."

"That voice! Reveal yourself!" Adam shouts.

Lucifer reveals himself and stands before Adam.

"What did you do with Charlie?" Adam demands.

"Charlie, that pathetic human, is still at the monastery."

"What?"

"You heard me. I left him there, and you're lucky he's still in one piece. How I would have loved to destroy him, but it would have been too easy. As soon as I heard that you were returning, I knew I had to accompany you back here myself."

"Why are you doing this to me?"

"Because I want what is rightfully mine."

"And what would that be?"

"You. I have come for you."

"I'm not ready to die."

"Maybe not, but I am going to assist you with that." Lucifer moves closer to Adam and begins to create a ball of fire in his hands. Seeing this, Adam steps back. Lucifer smiles and is about to send the ball of fire at him, when Michael suddenly appears and launches a ball of light—a direct hit on Lucifer. Lucifer falls and looks up at Michael. Adam is shocked and amazed.

"Michael, you have no business here," says Lucifer angrily. "Leave."

"You have no right to take this mortal's life."

"Why are you meddling in my personal affairs?" Lucifer yells.

"God has sent me. He has been watching you and is very displeased with your choice of actions."

"Oh, really? I don't see why. I am doing what is right."

Michael turns and looks at Adam. "Adam, God has not forsaken you. He sees everything. He is aware of all his children, and you should never doubt his love."

"Don't listen to Michael," says Lucifer. "He lies. The only reason God knows you is because of me. Listen to me. What do you think happens to you when you die? Do you think God will be there waiting to greet you? No, Adam, God won't be there. You have to earn the right to see him, and not everybody that dies gets that chance. It's a matter of luck, really."

Adam looks at Michael and then turns back to Lucifer.

"You lie!" yells Adam. "Why else would God have sent Michael to protect me from you?"

"Believe what you want, Adam, but I speak the truth. You know I will be there in the end. In fact, I want to take you now and spare you the hard life that awaits you. You will never be able to redeem yourself and remove my mark. Accept your fate, and come with me."

"No!" Adam shouts at him. "I believe that God thinks I may still have a chance."

"And you do," says Michael as he approaches Adam. "Believe me, our Messiah wants to help you."

"Adam, what's going on here?" It is Charlie's voice that grabs Adam's attention. "Why didn't you wait for me? Who are you talking to?"

Adam turns to see Charlie moving toward him. "Charlie! How did you find me?"

"I remembered the direction you told me you'd gone, and I ran after you. What's going on?" Charlie suddenly takes notice of Michael and Lucifer. "Oh my God, I can't believe this. You were right!"

"What's the matter, Charlie?" asks Lucifer, smiling. "Didn't you think I was real?"

"Pay no attention to Lucifer," says Michael. "Take Adam and leave this place."

Hearing this, Lucifer is furious. He creates a ball of flame in his hands and launches it at Adam. Adam is hit, and Michael turns to attack Lucifer with his sword. Lucifer sends more balls of fire at Michael, who flies into the air to avoid being hit.

"Adam, are you all right?" asks Charlie.

"I'm fine. He got me on my arm."

"Adam, I can't believe I'm seeing this. I'm sorry I doubted you. It seems to me that he really wants you."

"I'm scared," says Adam. "I have a bad feeling about this."

Lucifer and Michael continue fighting, neither of them backing down. "Give up, Michael," Lucifer yells. "Adam belongs to me!"

"Adam is not yours yet," Michael insists.

"Michael, let's stop this fighting. There's no need for this. You know as well as I do that I won fair and square."

Lucifer turns to see Charlie helping Adam up. He creates another ball of fire and sends it flying at Charlie. Adam sees the ball coming at Charlie and pushes him out of the way. The fiery sphere hits Adam directly in the chest.

When Lucifer sees this, he begins to laugh. "I win!" he yells.

Michael turns and looks at Charlie, who is holding Adam in his arms.

"You've failed, Michael," Lucifer gloats. "Adam is mine."

"It's still not over." Michael turns to the sky and calls out to God. "God, help me! Come to my aid!"

Lucifer approaches Charlie and smiles. "I know what sinful deeds you too have committed, and believe me, I will be waiting for you."

"You don't frighten me, you demon," Charlie shouts. "Go back to hell!"

Michael walks toward Lucifer. Charlie, who is holding Adam, begins to cry. "Adam, wake up! You can't die. You saved me."

Lucifer says, "Don't think that just because Adam sacrificed his life to save you, he will be redeemed and go to heaven, where God will welcome him with open arms. It doesn't work that way." In the silence, he realizes that Michael is nearby. "Isn't that right, Michael? One good deed can never redeem a mortal sinner—especially one who has committed all seven deadly sins."

Lucifer turns to shove Charlie into Michael, as he grabs Adam by the hand. Slowly the ground beneath Adam begins to open up, and Lucifer and Adam disappear into the underworld.

Michael calls out frantically to Charlie as he starts to follow Lucifer. "Come on, Charlie, before the ground seals itself up. Don't you want to help him?"

"No, Michael, I fear for my soul. What's going to happen to Adam?"

Michael sees that Charlie is in shock and frozen in place. He walks over and tries to comfort him. "Charlie, what happened to Adam was unfortunate. It is a sad loss to us all. But you have to understand that with his death will come a new beginning."

Charlie takes a look around and walks to where Adam once lay. "I don't understand how God can let this happen after he sent you to save Adam. Why didn't other angels come to help you?"

"One day you will come to realize God's plan, but until that day comes, you must remain strong. God will never forget you or any mortal that works to spread his gospel."

Charlie hears a sound above them and looks up to see angels descending from the sky.

"We still have a chance to save Adam," says Michael.

"How is that possible? He has Lucifer's seal. I saw it with my own eyes."

"Listen," says Michael, "every human has a chance at salvation, no matter what sins he has committed. God offers forgiveness, and if you truly believe in him with all your heart and soul, you will be saved. You need to have faith and absolute trust in him. You cannot be afraid of the one who has made you. He does not want humans to fear him but to love him."

Feeling guilty, Charlie looks at the ground and shakes his head in disbelief. "What are we going to do?" he asks sadly.

Michael looks at Charlie and points his sword at the sky. "We are going to save him. He called out to God before he was taken. He sounded sincere, and in the end, God has the final say on where a soul goes after it is released from the body. He's not just your Creator, but ours as well."

An angel of light approaches Michael with a concerned expression and interrupts their conversation.

"Michael, we must hurry. The ground below is slowly closing."

"God really hears us?" asks Charlie.

Michael nods at the angel, looks at the closing ground, and continues to speak. "Yes, God hears everything. You cannot hide any sin, any foul comment, anything at all. He is always watching his creation."

"I'm afraid," says Charlie. "I don't think I can do this."

"You have God and me by your side. There is nothing you should fear."

"What if I go with you and die in hell? Does that mean I will be dead in this world?"

"Do not fear death. Embrace it. Remember that this mortal world is not really your home. It is only temporary. Your real home is in the heavens with our Creator. He does not want you to get attached to mortal luxuries. You have to keep in mind that you cannot take any belonging with you."

Charlie takes hold of the cross hanging on his chest and squeezes it tight. "But why?" he asks.

"Because he already has a place waiting for you in his kingdom. So why would you need anything if it's already provided for you?"

Fearful, Charlie closes his eyes. Michael, concerned that the ground is closing, tells the angel to go on ahead. "It is your decision to join us and fight," he says to Charlie, "or to stay here and wait for my return."

Charlie sees a reddish glow in the ground where the other angels are entering. "He sacrificed his life to save me," he says. "I should be dead and lying on the ground. It should have been me. Why would he sacrifice his life to save me?" Charlie takes a deep breath. He looks up at the sky and then down at the ground below. "I have no choice. I have to help save him. After all, he would do the same for me, and he has." Charlie holds on to the cross around his neck and yells, "Let's go!"

"Are you sure?" asks Michael. "I don't want to pressure you."

"I have to do this."

"Very well, then." Michael hands Charlie a sword. "You're going to need this in case we get separated. Be careful not to touch anything. They will try to tempt you with mortal desires, but remember that God is always with you. Don't be afraid, and no matter what happens, never lose your faith. Never doubt our Messiah."

"Tempt me? How?" Charlie asks, following Michael toward the opening in the ground. "What have I gotten myself into? And what's that smell?"

"It is sulfur," Michael says.

"And listen to those horrible screams, dear God, protect me," Yells Charlie

Michael nods in agreement. "God protect us all."